TRENDS IN CYBERSECURITY THE INSIDER TO INSIDER RISKS

BY
DEVRAJ GANGULY

ISBN 978-93-5438-366-3
© DEVRAJ GANGULY 2020
Published in India 2020 by Pencil

A brand of
One Point Six Technologies Pvt. Ltd.
123, Building J2, Shram Seva Premises,
Wadala Truck Terminal, Wadala (E)
 Mumbai 400037, Maharashtra, INDIA
E connect@thepencilapp.com
W www.thepencilapp.com

Author biography

This book is written by DEVRAJ GANGULY. I have worked with renowned companies like Microsoft and IBM. I am a student Ambassador of CLIFFORD CHANCE LLP and JP MORGAN CHASE AND CO.

Contents

Preface

FOUR ASPECTS ALWAYS ARISE WHENEVER YOU THINK ABOUT A PARTICULAR ROPIC LIKE

1.   AN IDEA

2.   2 .AN APPROACH

3.   3 .A TOOL

4.   4. AND A CONCEPT.

5.   First of all idea will be given to write any book or chapter then we come to the approach.The objectives of approach are to control the variables affecting the process in an effective manner. The approach involves the series of stages.

6.   The tool is simply a control chart. Quality improvements are a result of a concept.

7.   I have tried my level best as a writer to impart all the impart the knowledge that I have so that it helps the beginners a lot.

8.   THIS IS MY FIRST BOOK.

9.   DEVRAJ GANGULY

Introduction

I Am Devraj Ganguly. I Am A Student But Also A Cyber Security Analyst As Acclaimed By Ibm And Cyberark.

I Was An Intern At Microsoft From December 2019 Till May 2020.

I Was A Student Ambassador At Clifford Chance Llp Frpom June 2020 Till September 2020

I Am Currently The Student Ambassador At Jp Morgan Chase And Co. And A Full Time Coder At Hackerrank.

1

WHAT IS CYBERSECURITY

Cyber security is the practice of defending computers, servers, mobile devices, electronic systems, networks, and data from malicious attacks. It's also known as information technology security or electronic information security. The term applies in a variety of contexts, from business to mobile computing, and can be divided into a few common categories.

Cyber threats are a global risk that governments, the private sector, non-governmental organizations – and the global community as a whole – must deal with. Chatham House aims to build cyber capacity and expertise among policymakers, via International Security programme 's Cyber Policy Portfolio.

The world of cybersecurity is never a dull one. Thousands of news and articles about the latest trends in technology are published every day, it's almost impossible to catch up. In a sea of tech blogs claiming to feature relevant news and engaging topics, we understand if you're having a hard time choosing one .

This focuses on building cyber capacity and expertise among policymakers, investigating key issues through publishing in-depth policy research, conducting cyber simulation exercises, and convening high-level meetings with a wide group of stakeholders.

The programme also produces the highly-respected *Journal of Cyber Policy* , a unique place for scholars and practitioners to address emerging cyber policy challenges.

1. **WHAT ARE THE DIFFERENT PHASES OF SECURITY**

   Network security is the practice of securing a computer network from intruders, whether targeted attackers or opportunistic malware

   Application security focuses on keeping software and devices free of threats. A compromised application could provide access to the data its designed to protect. Successful security begins in the design stage, well before a program or device is deployed.

Information security protects the integrity and privacy of data, both in storage and in transit.

Operational security includes the processes and decisions for handling and protecting data assets. The permissions users have when accessing a network and the procedures that determine how and where data may be stored or shared all fall under this umbrella.

Disaster recovery and business continuity define how an organization responds to a cyber-security incident or any other event that causes the loss of operations or data. Disaster recovery policies dictate how the organization restores its operations and information to return to the same operating capacity as before the event. Business continuity is the plan the organization falls back on while trying to operate without certain resources.

End-user education addresses the most unpredictable cyber-security factor: people. Anyone can accidentally introduce a virus to an otherwise secure system by failing to follow good security practices. Teaching users to delete suspicious email attachments, not plug in unidentified USB drives, and various other important lessons is vital for the security of any organization.

2. THE SCALE OF CYBER THREAT.

The global cyber threat continues to evolve at a rapid pace, with a rising number of data breaches each year. A report by Risk Based Security . revealed that a shocking 7.9 billion records have been exposed by data breaches in the first nine months of 2019 alone. This figure is more than double (112%) the number of records exposed in the same period in 2018.

Medical services, retailers and public entities experienced the most breaches, with malicious criminals responsible for most incidents. Some of these sectors are more appealing to cybercriminals because they collect financial and medical data, but all businesses that use networks can be targeted for customer data, corporate espionage, or customer attacks

With the scale of the cyber threat set to continue to rise, the International Data Corporation predicts that worldwide spending on cyber-security solutions will reach a massive $133.7 billion by 2022. Governments across the globe have responded to the rising cyber threat with guidance to help organizations implement effective cyber-security practices.

In the U.S., the National Institute of Standards and Technology (NIST) has created a cyber-security framework . To combat the proliferation of malicious code and aid in early detection, the framework recommends continuous, real-time monitoring of all electronic resources.

The importance of system monitoring is echoed in the " 10 steps to cyber security ", guidance provided by the U.K. government's National Cyber Security Centre. In Australia, The Australian Cyber Security Centre (ACSC) regularly publishes guidance on how organizations can counter the latest cyber-security threats.

3. THE TYPES OF CYBER THREATS:

The threats countered by cyber-security are three-fold

1. **Cybercrime**   includes single actors or groups targeting systems for financial gain or to cause disruption.

2. **Cyber-attack** often involves politically motivated information gathering.

3. **Cyberterrorism** is intended to undermine electronic systems to cause panic or fear.

So, how do malicious actors gain control of computer systems? Here are some common methods used to threaten cyber-security:

Malware:

Malware means malicious software. One of the most common cyber threats, malware is software that a cybercriminal or hacker has created to disrupt or damage a legitimate user's computer. Often spread via an unsolicited email attachment or legitimate-looking download, malware may be used by cybercriminals to make money or in politically motivated cyber-attacks.

There are a number of different types of malware, including:

Virus: A self-replicating program that attaches itself to clean file and spreads throughout a computer system, infecting files with malicious code.

Trojans : A type of malware that is disguised as legitimate software. Cybercriminals trick users into uploading Trojans onto their computer where they cause damage or collect data.

Spyware: A program that secretly records what a user does, so that cybercriminals can make use of this information. For example, spyware could capture credit card details.

Ransomware: Malware which locks down a user's files and data, with the threat of erasing it unless a ransom is paid.

Adware: Advertising software which can be used to spread malware.

Botnets: Networks of malware infected computers which cybercriminals use to perform tasks online without the user's permission.

SQL injection:

An SQL (structured language query) injection is a type of cyber-attack used to take control of and steal data from a database. Cybercriminals exploit vulnerabilities in data-driven applications to insert malicious code into a databased via a malicious SQL statement. This gives them access to the sensitive information contained in the database.

Phishing:

Phishing is when cybercriminals target victims with emails that appear to be from a legitimate company asking for sensitive information. Phishing attacks are often used to dupe people into handing over credit card data and other personal information.

Man-in-the-middle attack:

A man-in-the-middle attack is a type of cyber threat where a cybercriminal intercepts communication between two individuals in order to steal data. For example, on an unsecure WiFi network, an attacker could intercept data being passed from the victim's device and the network.

Denial-of-service attack:

A denial-of-service attack is where cybercriminals prevent a computer system from fulfilling legitimate requests by overwhelming the networks and servers with traffic. This renders the system unusable, preventing an organization from carrying out vital functions.

Latest cyber threats

What are the latest cyber threats that individuals and organizations need to guard against? Here are some of the most recent cyber threats that the U.K., U.S., and Australian governments have reported on.

Dridex malware

In December 2019, the U.S. Department of Justice (DoJ) charged the leader of an organized cyber-criminal group for their part in a global Dridex malware attack . This malicious campaign affected the public, government, infrastructure and business worldwide.

Dridex is a financial trojan with a range of capabilities. Affecting victims since 2014, it infects computers though phishing emails or existing malware. Capable of stealing passwords, banking details and personal data which can be used in fraudulent transactions, it has caused massive financial losses amounting to hundreds of millions.

In response to the Dridex attacks, the U.K.'s National Cyber Security Centre advises the public to "ensure devices are patched, anti-virus is turned on and up to date and files are backed up"

Romance scams:

In February 2020, the FBI warned U.S. citizens to be aware of confidence fraud that cybercriminals commit using dating sites, chat rooms and apps. Perpetrators take advantage of people seeking new partners, duping victims into giving away personal data. The FBI reports that romance cyber threats affected 114 victims in New Mexico in 2019, with financial losses amounting to $1.6 million.

Emotet malware:

In late 2019, The Australian Cyber Security Centre warned national organizations about a widespread global cyber threat from Emotet malware.

Emotet is a sophisticated trojan that can steal data and also load other malware. Emotet thrives on unsophisticated password: a reminder of the importance of creating a secure password to guard against cyber threats.

End-user protection

End-user protection or endpoint security is a crucial aspect of cyber security. After all, it is often an individual (the end-user) who accidentally uploads malware or another form of cyber threat to their desktop, laptop or mobile device.

So, how do cyber-security measures protect end users and systems? First, cyber-security relies on cryptographic protocols to encrypt emails, files, and other critical data. This not only protects information in transit, but also guards against loss or theft.

In addition, end-user security software scans computers for pieces of malicious code, quarantines this code, and then removes it from the machine. Security programs can even detect and remove malicious code hidden in primary boot record and are designed to encrypt or wipe data from computer's hard drive.

Electronic security protocols also focus on real-time malware detection . Manse heuristic and behavioral analysis to monitor the behavior of a program and its code to defend against viruses or Trojans that change their shape with each execution (polymorphic and metamorphic malware). Security programs can confine potentially malicious programs to a virtual bubble separate from a user's network to analyze their behavior and learn how to better detect new infections.

Security programs continue to evolve new defenses as cyber-security professionals identify new threats and new ways to combat them. To make the most of end-user security software, employees need to be educated about how to use it. Crucially, keeping it running and updating it frequently ensures that it can protect users against the latest cyber threats

Cyber safety tips - protect yourself against cyberattacks

How can businesses and individuals guard against cyber threats? Here are our top cyber safety tips:

1. **Update your software and operating system:** This means you benefit from the latest security patches.

2. **Use anti-virus software:** Security solutions like Kaspersky Total Security will detect and removes threats. Keep your software updated for the best level of protection.

3. **Use strong passwords:** Ensure your passwords are not easily guessable.

4. **Do not open email attachments from unknown senders:** These could be infected with malware.

5. **Do not click on links in emails from unknown senders or unfamiliar websites:** This is a common way that malware is spread.

6. Avoid using unsecure WiFi networks in public places: Unsecure networks leave you vulnerable to man-in-the-middle attacks.

Internet Safety: How to Protect Yourself Against Hackers: Recent reports estimate that there will be between 20 and 30 billion Internet-connected devices by 2020. Many people are familiar with computers, tablets, smartphones, and wireless Internet. Now other "smart" devices, like televisions, home security cameras, and even refrigerators, connect to the Internet. More devices mean more avenues for attack by hackers.

What is Hacking?

Hackers illegally access devices or websites to steal peoples' personal information, which they use to commit the crimes like theft. Many people shop, bank, and pay bills online. People also store financial information, like credit card or bank account numbers, on their devices. A hacker can do a lot of damage even if only one account or device is compromised. To make matters worse, hackers are difficult to stop because they are often located outside the United States and use cutting edge technology to evade law enforcement and acquire large amounts of information.

There are two main ways hackers may try to get your personal information. One way is to try to obtain information directly from an Internet-connected device by installing spyware, which sends information from your device to others without your knowledge or consent. Hackers may install spyware by tricking you into opening spam email, or into "clicking" on attachments, images, and links in email messages, instant messages, and pop-up messages. Hackers use spyware to track keystrokes or acquire pictures of your device's screen in the hope of snagging account numbers, passwords, and other sensitive information. Criminals can also hack individual websites—like email, social media, or financial institutions—and steal the information stored there. While trying to protect all your devices and accounts from these criminals may seem daunting, there are some easy, practical steps you can take to keep your information more secure.

Protecting Computers and Laptops

Make sure your security software is up-to-date. Devices' operating systems and Internet-connected software (like email programs, web browsers, and music players) should be updated regularly. Your computer will typically notify you when a software update is available.

Install antivirus and antimalware software. If you do not have security software, install a firewall and antivirus software and keep them up-to-date. There are a variety of reputable products available for free or that have a free trial period. These programs help identify the latest threats and allow a user to remove malicious software from their device. Do your research before installing any program and beware of scams that attempt to lure you into disclosing your personal information or that direct you to download programs that may contain malware.

Disable connections when you aren't using them. If your computer uses Wi-Fi or Bluetooth to connect to the Internet and other devices, you should turn these features off when you aren't using them. This can prevent unknown persons from using your network or accessing your devices without your knowledge.

Protecting Cell Phones

Create a strong PIN or passcode. If your device is lost or stolen, a strong passcode may prevent a thief from accessing all the information stored on your phone. Many smartphones also allow you to remotely wipe the information from your computer in the event of loss or theft.

Only install trusted applications. Some criminals make available applications (or "apps") that look and function like legitimate apps, but actually install malware to your smartphone. Be sure to download apps only from trusted sources, and check the number of downloads and read reviews to makes sure you aren't downloading a "look-alike" app.

Keep your software up-to-date. Smartphone manufacturers and app developers regularly release software updates that often include security improvements. Check often to ensure that your smartphone has the most up-to-date software.

Protecting Other Internet-Connected Devices

As mentioned above, Internet-connected televisions and appliances are now available in the marketplace. These devices, as well as the router that connects your home to the Internet, are also vulnerable to attack. It is important to protect these devices just like computers and smartphones.

Review your network and device names. Is your cell phone or home network named using your last name or other personally identifying information? This can make your device more vulnerable to attack, since it connects the device to you and makes it easier for hackers to guess your password. You should change the name of your devices and network so hackers cannot identify you so easily.

Create unique passwords for all devices. When you purchase a new device, it often comes with a simple, default password. Many people set up unique passwords for their computer or phone, but neglect to do so for their Internet router or other smart device. Unknown to the user, hackers can easily gain access to these devices, and use them to flood websites with so much traffic the site goes down or hack into your network. If, for example, your "smart" kitchen stove is connected to the Internet and has a simple password, a hacker could use the stove to access your wireless network and hack your computer or phone. When you get a new Internet-connected device, you should be sure to create a strong, unique password for it.

Protecting Online Accounts

Delete suspicious emails. It is best to delete spam or dubious-looking emails without opening them. If you receive a questionable email from a friend or family member, it is best to contact that person and verify he or she sent it before opening the email or clicking on a link or attachment.

Use secure devices. If possible, only access online accounts from your personal computer, tablet, or smartphone while using a secured Internet connection. Try to limit accessing personal accounts from public computers that could be infected with spyware or malware, or may use an unsecured Internet connection. If you do use public computers, be sure to log out when you are finished. In general, it is more secure to use a smartphone's cellular data network than a public or unsecured Internet connection.

Create strong passwords. To reduce the chances of your online accounts being hacked, change your passwords frequently. Strong passwords are at least 12 characters long, include numbers, letters, special characters (&,!,?, etc.), and are not too predictable. For example, don't use your name or date of birth for your password or common words like "password." If you have multiple online accounts, it is best to have a different password for each account. In the event that one of your accounts is hacked, having different passwords for your other accounts reduces the likelihood of those accounts being accessed too.

Use multifactor authentication on your accounts. Multifactor authentication works like this: When you enter your password for your email account, for example, you are directed to a page that asks for a four-digit code. Your email provider then sends a unique, temporary code in a text message or to another email account. You must enter the code, which expires after a short amount of time, to access your account. This means that hackers who obtained your password still can't access your account unless they also have access to that verification code, adding another layer of protection. Many email providers, social media websites, and financial institutions now make it easy for users to set up multifactor authentication on their accounts.

Be cautious with "Save my information for next time." Many websites now store personal banking or credit card information to make it easier for you to buy a product or to pay a bill in the future. Although convenient, if your account is hacked, your payment information is more easily available to hackers. Ensure any website where you enter your financial information is secure (the website's URL should start with "https://"—remember that the "s" is for "secure"), that your password is unique to that account, and that you log out once you are done.

Sign up for account alerts. Many email providers and social media websites allow users to sign up for an email or text alert when your account is accessed from a new device or unusual location. These email or text alerts can quickly notify you when an unauthorized person accesses your account and can help minimize the amount of time an unauthorized user has access to your information. If you receive such an alert, login to your account immediately and change the password. Check these emails closely, however, since malicious "phishing" emails often mimic these kinds of alerts.

If Your Device or Online Accounts are Hacked

Have devices inspected. If your computer or other device is hacked, disconnect it from the Internet and have it looked at and repaired by a trusted specialist. Be cautious when calling telephone numbers for technical support specialists that you find online. Scam artists sometimes set up authentic-looking websites that may appear to be affiliated with your computer's manufacturer. When consumers call these entities, they are often told they must pay hundreds of dollars for their computer to be fixed, or the "technician" installs other viruses onto the computer that steal information or cause more problems. It is often best to take the device to a physical repair shop, rather than trying to find a technician online. If you call a technician online, be sure to research the company and its phone number to be sure it is legitimate.

Change your passwords. After getting a device repaired or cleaned of viruses, you should change all the passwords for any accounts you accessed using the device. The malicious software that was removed from your computer may have transmitted your passwords to an attacker, granting the hacker easy access to your information. Similarly, if one of your online accounts has been hacked, be sure to change your password immediately. A hacker may also change your password, denying you access to the account. If you are unable to access your account, contact the website directly and it can assist you in restoring your account.

Monitor financial accounts. If a hacked account contains financial information, contact your bank or credit card company immediately, letting it know that your account may be compromised. Your bank or credit card company may issue you a new card or account number. Be sure to monitor activity on the account for any fraudulent transactions. In some cases, hackers may have obtained your information, but will not use it right away. If you are not issued a new card or account number, you should monitor your account for an extended period.

Notify others. When appropriate, contact your friends and family and make them aware your device or account has been hacked. Hackers may try to gain access to your email contact list, and send emails from your account. Notifying friends and family that your account has been hacked, and instructing them not to open urgent or strange emails, "click" on suspicious links, or download attachments that seem to come from you may help protect their accounts from hackers.

Watch out for other users. People often are not immediately aware that their email or social media accounts have been hacked. In fact, many people only learn of the problem when friends or family contact them about a suspicious email or message from their account. If something doesn't seem right about a person's email or social media account, it is possible the account was hacked. Do not respond to any emails or messages you receive, but contact your friend or family member directly and tell them about the problem.

5 THINGS TO KNOW BEFORE GETTING STARTED IN CYBERSECURITY:

1. Cyber is a very broad church: Cyber has exploded. Back when I was a kid it was a bunch of hanging out on IRC and visiting Vegas. The idea you would hire a hacker was laughable to most people. It was a small culture of generalists. At my first job, an oil company, whenever I talked about deploying virus software they would ask me if I meant "anti-virus" software. Yes. Because that was my job. But they were convinced it meant something bad.

Nowadays, some organisations have Risk teams, you have Policy, you have red teams trying to break into companies, you have people sat looking at Splunk trying to figure out what is happening to defend their organisations.

It's worth keeping in mind most every conversation you have internally in departments will be with somebody who looks at something in a specific way. It's also worth keeping in mind this with online conversations, too. Lots of conversations online go something like "Just patch!". Which, from a policy point of view, is absolutely right. From the point of view of the people who actually do the patching at scale and manage the systems operationally, "Just patch!" is a bit like saying "Just phone up Taylor Swift and ask her to be your friend".

2. The security community is pretty terrible at times Back in my youth(tm), we would hang on IRC all day, and then meet up at night for drinks. People knew each other's real life infos when they met. Trusts were formed. Ideas were exchanged. And, well, lots of idiots were   around too.

Many of those people got jobs at big companies, or left the industry.

What is left is a weird shell with lots of different angles. Some of it is brilliant. I like InfoSec Twitter, for example, most of the time as I see material I wouldn't otherwise. I read almost no InfoSec websites; I exist off a diet of animated GIFs and info drops. I try to never take it seriously.

But there's a weird atmosphere. I think the Infosec community has gradually eroded, and in it's place there's a weird dynamic of self importance emerging, especially post WannaCry as companies seek to find talent.

3. Prepare to earn your place Lots of people are arriving into cybersecurity. Which is great because fresh people and ideas are absolutely needed — since I started many of the same problems still exist, which is embarrassing. I think there's a very real lack of diversity in every sense in our industry.

But here's the thing. I think the number one quality people can bring to the arena is also experience. That doesn't mean 10 years experience. That means existing in a job and a company and doing the hard work. If you're really in there, delivering, doing, you're going to be valuable and won't have problems finding other jobs in the future. Commit. Do. Deliver.

It's also worth pointing out many companies are still early in their cyber journey, and some need guidance. Sometimes, you may have to do things which you weren't expecting in a role. Sometimes, that's a bad sign. In many cases, it allows you to break free from the box you're in and get involved in something great. Sometimes you have to gamble and take the lead. My rule is that if you're doing something which truly aids an organisation in being secure, you're doing it right.

4. Write it. Shoot it. Publish it.Whatever BUT TRY TO MAKE IT OF YOUR OWN. This isn't for everyone, but if you're looking at getting into the industry, you can start a blog and write. Or learn to code and then publish said code.

You will be surprised how many basic tools in InfoSec still don't exist. For example, through its product life there was no easy central way to report on events from Microsoft EMET. Companies are doing things like associating .vbs files to Notepad as a way of mitigating ransomware attacks, but nobody has written a tool to do this better.

5. Have interests outside security: The burn out is real. You will hit a wall. So have interests outside security.

I play video games — which is older than most of the people I play against. I play games like GTA V , a game which requires patience along with skills. That's actually helped me with communication skills, as — for example — there's no on screen map, so you have to tell people which direction to sail in using compasses, and make sure people are motivated to continue otherwise they just quit.

* * *

2.

HACKERS VS CRACKERS

WHO AREHACKERS?

A computer **hacker** is a computer expert who uses their technical knowledge to achieve a goal or overcome an obstacle, within a computerized system by non-standard means.

Though the term "hacker" has become associated in popular culture with a "hacker security " – someone who utilizes their technical know-how of bugs or exploits to break into computer systems and access data which would otherwise be unavailable to them – hacking can also be utilized by legitimate figures in legal situations. For example, law enforcement agencies sometimes use hacking techniques in order to collect evidence on criminals and other malicious actors. This could include using anonymity tools (such as a VPN , or the dark web) to mask their identities online, posing as criminals themselves.   Likewise, covert world agencies can employ hacking techniques in the legal conduct of their work. Oppositely, hacking and cyber-attacks are used extra- and illegally by law enforcement and security agencies (conducting warrantless activities), and employed by State actors as a weapon of both legal and illegal warfare.

Reflecting the two types of hackers, there are two definitions of the word "hacker":

Originally, hacker simply meant advanced computer technology enthusiast (both hardware and software) and adherent of programming subculture;

Someone who is able to subvert computer security . If doing so for malicious purposes, the person can also be called a cracker.

Today, mainstream usage of "hacker" mostly refers to computer criminals, due to the mass media usage of the word since the 1990s.This includes what hacker slang calls "script kiddies", people breaking into computers using programs written by others, with very little knowledge about the way they work. This usage has become so predominant that the general public is largely unaware that different meanings exist.   While the self-designation of hobbyists as hackers is generally acknowledged and accepted by computer security hackers, people from the programming subculture consider the computer intrusion related usage incorrect, and emphasize the difference between the two by calling security breakers "crackers" (analogous to a safecracker).

The controversy is usually based on the assertion that the term originally meant someone messing about with something in a positive sense, that is, using playful cleverness to achieve a goal. But then, it is supposed, the meaning of the term shifted over the decades and came to refer to computer criminals.

As the security-related usage has spread more widely, the original meaning has become less known. In popular usage and in the media, "computer intruders" or "computer criminals" is the exclusive meaning of the word today. (For example, "An Internet 'hacker' broke through state government security systems in March.") In the computer enthusiast (Hacker Culture) community, the primary meaning is a complimentary description for a particularly brilliant programmer or technical expert. (For example, " Linus Torvalds , the creator of Linux , is considered by some to be a hacker."

Representation in mainstream media:

The mainstream media 's current usage of the term may be traced back to the early 1980s. When the term, previously used only among computer enthusiasts, was introduced to wider society by the mainstream media in 1983, even those in the computer community referred to computer intrusion as "hacking", although not as the exclusive definition of the word. In reaction to the increasing media use of the term exclusively with the criminal connotation, the computer community began to differentiate their terminology. Alternative terms such as "cracker" were coined in an effort to maintain the distinction between "hackers" within the legitimate programmer community and those performing computer break-ins. Further terms such as "black hat", "white hat" and "gray hat" developed when laws against breaking into computers came into effect, to distinguish criminal activities from those activities which were legal.

TYPES OF HACKERS:

White hat hacker: White hats are hackers who work to keep data safe from other hackers by finding system vulnerabilities   that can be mitigated. White hats are usually employed by the target system's owner and are typically paid (sometimes quite well) for their work. Their work is not illegal because it is done with the system owner's consent.

Black hat hacker: Black hats or crackers are hackers with malicious intentions. They often steal, exploit, and sell data, and are usually motivated by personal gain. Their work is usually illegal. A cracker is like a black hat hacker, but is specifically someone who is very skilled and tries via hacking to make profits or to benefit, not just to vandalize. Crackers find exploits for system vulnerabilities and often use them to their advantage by either selling the fix to the system owner or selling the exploit to other black hat hackers, who in turn use it to steal information or gain royalties.

Grey hat hacker: Grey hats include those who hack for fun or to troll . They may both fix and exploit vulnerabilities, but usually not for financial gain. Even if not malicious, their work can still be illegal, if done without the target system owner's consent, and grey hats are usually associated with black hat hackers.

Motives: Four primary motives have been proposed as possibilities for why hackers attempt to break into computers and networks. First, there is a criminal financial gain to be had when hacking systems with the specific purpose of stealing credit card numbers or manipulating banking systems . Second, many hackers thrive off of increasing their reputation within the hacker subculture and will leave their handles on websites they defaced or leave some other evidence as proof that they were involved in a specific hack. Third, corporate espionage allows companies to acquire information on products or services that can be stolen or used as leverage within the marketplace. And fourth, state-sponsored attacks provide nation states with both wartime and intelligence collection options conducted on, in, or through cyberspace.

Crackers: The members of the computer underground should be called crackers. Yet, those people see themselves as hackers and even try to include the views of Raymond in what they see as a wider hacker culture, a view that Raymond has harshly rejected. Instead of a hacker/cracker dichotomy, they emphasize a spectrum of different categories, such as white hat , grey hat , black hat and script kiddie . In contrast to Raymond, they usually reserve the term *cracker* for more malicious activity.

White hat : A white hat hacker breaks security for non-malicious reasons, either to test their own security system, perform penetration tests , or vulnerability assessments for a client - or while working for a security company which makes security software. The term is generally synonymous with ethical hacker , and the EC-Council, among others, have developed certifications, courseware, classes, and online training covering the diverse arena of ethical hacking.

Black hat : A black hat hacker is a hacker who "violates computer security for little reason beyond maliciousness or for personal gain" (Moore, 2005). The term was coined by Richard Stallman, to contrast the maliciousness of a criminal hacker versus the spirit of playfulness and exploration in hacker culture, or the ethos of the white hat hacker who performs hacking duties to identify places to repair or as a means of legitimate employment. Black hat hackers form the stereotypical, illegal hacking groups often portrayed in popular culture, and are "the epitome of all that the public fears in a computer criminal".

Grey hat : A grey hat hacker lies between a black hat and a white hat hacker. A grey hat hacker may surf the Internet and hack into a computer system for the sole purpose of notifying the administrator that their system has a security defect, for example. They may then offer to correct the defect for a fee. Grey hat hackers sometimes find the defect of a system and publish the facts to the world instead of a group of people. Even though grey hat hackers may not necessarily perform hacking for their personal gain, unauthorized access to a system can be considered illegal and unethical.

Elite hacker : A social status among hackers, *elite* is used to describe the most skilled. Newly discovered exploits circulate among these hackers. Elite groups such as Masters of Deception conferred a kind of credibility on their members.

Script kiddie : :A script kiddie (also known as a *skid* or *skiddie*) is an unskilled hacker who breaks into computer systems by using automated tools written by others (usually by other black hat hackers), hence the term script (i.e. a computer script that automates the hacking) kiddie (i.e. kid, child—an individual lacking knowledge and experience, immature), usually with little understanding of the underlying concept.

Security exploits : A security exploit is a prepared application that takes advantage of a known weakness. [31] Common examples of security exploits are SQL injection, cross-site scripting and cross-site request forgery which abuse security holes that may result from substandard programming practice. Other exploits would be able to be used through File Transfer Protocol (FTP), Hypertext Transfer Protocol (HTTP), PHP , SSH ,

Telnet and some Web pages. These are very common in Web site and Web domain hacking.

3

IMPORTANT PROGRAMMING LANGUAGES FOR CYBERSECURITY.

To start a career in cybersecurity, the best programming languages to know are:

JavaScript .

HTML *

Python .

C .

C++

Assembly .

PHP .

4

SKILLS REQUIRED FOR A RESPECTABLE JOB IN THE FIELD OF CYBERSECURITY.

The Top Skills Required for Cybersecurity Jobs

Problem-Solving Skills . ...

Technical Aptitude. ...

Knowledge of Security Across Various Platforms. ...

Attention to Detail. ...

Communication Skills. ...

Fundamental Computer Forensics Skills. ...

A Desire to Learn. ...An Understanding of Hacking.

* * *

BEST CERTIFICATIONS TO BOOST YOUR CAREER IN CYBERSECURITY

Certified Ethical Hacker (CEH)

CompTIA Security+

Certified Information System Security Professional (CISSP)

Certified Information Security Manager (CISM)

Certified Information Systems Auditor (CISA)

NIST Cybersecurity Framework (NCSF)

Certified Cloud Security Professional (CCSP)

Computer Hacking Forensic Investigator (CHFI)

Cisco Certified Network Associate (CCNA) Security

* * *